This book is dedicated
to *Paul Daneman,*

with happy memories

NN *&* FD

A BRUBAKER, FORD & FRIENDS BOOK,
an imprint of The Templar Company Limited

First published in the UK in 2011 by Templar Publishing,
The Granary, North Street, Dorking, Surrey, RH4 1DN, UK
www.templarco.co.uk

Unabridged text originally published in 1983 by Heinemann/Quixote
This abridged text copyright © 2011 Bryan Forbes Ltd.
Illustration copyright © 2011 Flora Daneman

First edition

ISBN 978-1-84877-478-0

Printed in China

THAT DOG !

Nanette Newman

Illustrated by

Flora Daneman

With love
Nanette

B∥F∥&∥F

BRUBAKER, FORD & FRIENDS

AN IMPRINT OF THE TEMPLAR COMPANY LIMITED

"THAT DOG'S
barking again," said
Mrs Higgs crossly,
looking over the
fence that separated
the two gardens.

"He's not," said
Ben. "He's talking."

"Sounds like
barking to me," said
Mrs Higgs.

"Come on, Barney,"
Ben called. "Come
and help me tidy
my room."

"Ridiculous,"
snorted Mrs Higgs.

One morning, Mrs Higgs was standing by her front door when Barney and Ben were leaving.

"That dog's been digging up my garden."

"He's trying to be helpful, Mrs Higgs," said Ben. "I think he knows it's difficult for you to dig."

"He's snarling," she said.

"He's smiling," said Ben. "He's just happy."

"Huh!" said Mrs Higgs, who never looked happy, ever.

Ben and Barney had been together for as long as Ben could remember and Ben had taught him everything he knew.

"Sit," said Ben.

Barney just wagged his tail.

"That dog can't do anything," said Mrs Higgs.

"He can do tricks," said Ben.
   "What sort of tricks?" asked Mrs Higgs.
   "HUG!" said Ben, and Barney stood up and put his paws on Mrs Higgs' shoulders.
   "Get him off!" screamed Mrs Higgs.

"You call that a trick?" she said, running up the path.
   "Definitely," said Ben.

Sometimes Ben and Barney would spend quiet evenings together reading. Ben would read aloud to Barney, and Barney would put his head in Ben's lap and quietly concentrate on the story. His favourite was *Peter Pan*.

He liked the bit where Wendy sang to the Lost Boys best.

"That dog's whining," shouted Ben's mother from downstairs.

"He's singing," said Ben.

Barney wasn't allowed to be fed when the family were having supper. He would sit by Ben's chair and try to look sad and hungry, but Ben's mother would say: "You are not to feed him food off your plate, Ben."

"No, Mother," said Ben, with his fingers crossed under the table.

One day, when Ben and Barney were out shopping, Mrs Higgs started shouting: "Get that dog away from my basket."

"Mrs Higgs," said Ben patiently. "He's simply offering to carry it home for you."

"Rubbish!" said Mrs Higgs, as she walked away with her cross face.

Mrs Higgs was waiting for them when they got home.

"That dog…" she said.

"Do you mean Barney?" said Ben.

"That dog stole the lamb chops from my basket."

"Never," said Ben. "Mrs Higgs, does Barney look like a thief?"

Barney sat wagging his tail and panting.

"Yes," said Mrs Higgs.

"That woman," said Ben to Barney as they sat in the garden, "has no heart."

Barney agreed and licked the last bit of lamb chop from around his mouth.

Every night, Barney slept in Ben's room. When Ben's mother came in to say goodnight, Barney would be lying on his blanket in the corner.

The minute the door was closed he was on the bed, snuggled up to Ben.

Barney always cried when Ben was told off, listened when Ben had a problem and loved Ben as much as Ben loved him.

Then one day, Barney died.

"He was getting old," said Ben's mother, gently.

"He wasn't," said Ben, crying.

"He had a great life," said Ben's father.

"He didn't suffer," said the vet. "He'd just had a long and happy life; it was time for him to go. It happens to us all."

"But I didn't want it to happen to Barney," said Ben.

"I know," said the vet.

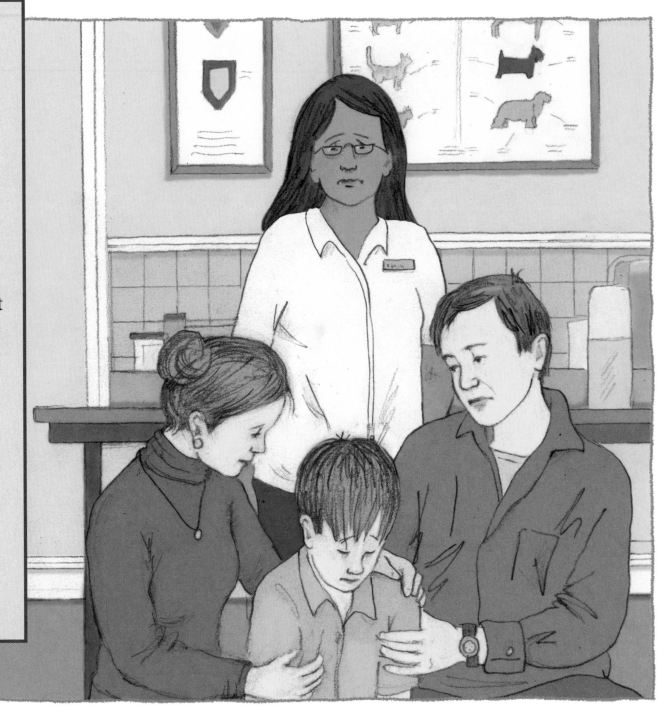

Ben gave Barney a grave in the garden and his father said a prayer or two. Then Ben read Barney's favourite bit from *Peter Pan*.

Mrs Higgs looked over the fence. She gave Ben the best rose from her garden to put on Barney's grave. She didn't have a cross look on her either.

"Thank you," said Ben.

Ben felt as if his heart had been broken. He would cry at night when he put out his hand on the bed, forgetting Barney wasn't there.

Ben's father said, "How about us getting another dog?"

"Never!" said Ben. "I never want another dog. Not ever."

At school, Ben's friend said, "Barney would have hated you to be sad. Think of him with happy thoughts, not sad ones."

One day when Ben was sitting behind the apple tree at the end of the garden, he heard a whimper. He stood up and walked to the long grass at the back of the shed, and there, almost hidden was a tiny puppy.

Ben stared, and so did the puppy.

He then came and sat on Ben's foot. Ben looked at him.

"I'm lost," the puppy seemed to say.

Ben looked around. There was no one about.

He picked up the puppy. There was no collar on him, and he seemed too young to be out on his own.

"What am I to do with you?" Ben said.

The puppy fell asleep in his arms.

Ben took him into the house.

"I suppose I'd better keep you until we find out who you belong to," he said.

The puppy seemed to like Ben's room.
He ate a slipper…

and tore up a book.

The days went by, but no one claimed him.

"I suppose we'll have to take him to the Dog's Home," said his mother.

"Tomorrow," said Ben.

He made a puddle on the floor, but when Ben explained to him that those habits were meant for the garden, he seemed to understand.

That night Ben sat in his room trying to paint a picture.

The puppy woke up and got off his foot.

He looked at Ben, trying to get him to play.

"I could never love another dog the way I loved Barney," said Ben. The puppy looked at him as if to say; "I know but you might love me in a different way."

Ben looked at him for a long time.

"I'll never forget Barney," said Ben.

"I know," the puppy seemed to say,

"but I need somebody to love me, too."

"Perhaps we could remember Barney

together," said Ben.

The puppy wagged his tail.

So that is what they did.

"**G**ood morning,
Mrs Higgs,"
said Ben.
"Oh, no! Not
another one!"
said Mrs Higgs.
"And what sort
of dog is that,
may I ask?"

"THAT, Mrs Higgs, is a very special sort of dog," said Ben as he and Bertie walked down the road together.